Pet Show Disaster!

'Pet Show Disaster!'
An original concept by Elizabeth Dale
© Elizabeth Dale

Illustrated by Veronica Montoya

Published by MAVERICK ARTS PUBLISHING LTD

Studio 11, City Business Centre, 6 Brighton Road,

Horsham, West Sussex, RH13 5BB

© Maverick Arts Publishing Limited August 2020

+44 (0)1403 256941

A CIP catalogue record for this book is available at the British Library.

ISBN 978-1-84886-694-2

www.maverickbooks.co.uk

This book is rated as: Turquoise Band (Guided Reading)

Pet Show Disaster!

by Elizabeth Dale

illustrated by
Veronica Montoya

Jenny loved Jasper. He was the best pet in the whole world. He always rushed to wake her up in the morning.

Jasper always knew how Jenny was feeling.

When she was sad, he snuggled up to her.

When she was happy, he jumped and

wagged his tail. They had such fun together!

GRAND
PET SHOW!

One day, Jenny saw a notice.

"Look Jasper!" Jenny cried. "You are the best pet in the world. You could win the Pet Show!"

Jasper woofed happily. He thought he could win too!

Jenny helped Jasper practise for the Pet Show. She made an obstacle course for him to run round.

Jenny taught Jasper to sit and stay and come. And Jasper did just what Jenny told him – most of the time!

"Well done, Jasper!" Jenny said, hugging him. "You're a star!"

Soon it was the day before the show. Jasper ran round Jenny's obstacle course very fast. "Good boy!" Jenny cried. "Now I just need to make you even more beautiful."

Jasper woofed happily. But then

he heard Jenny filling the bath.

So Jasper raced down the garden and hid!

"Come on, Jasper!" Jenny laughed.

She took him back inside.

"Don't you want to win at the show?

Look, the water is lovely and warm."

Jasper hated baths.

He howled as Jenny washed him!

As soon as she'd finished, he shook

himself dry – all over her.

Jenny laughed and dried them both.

Then she brushed Jasper's long fur.

"There, you're beautiful now," she said.

Jasper wagged his tail. Then he went outside and rolled in the mud!

"Oh Jasper!" Jenny cried. "Now I have to bath you all over again!"

Jenny was so excited she could hardly sleep that night. Next morning, Jasper wanted to play. He brought Jenny his ball.

"We'll have to play inside," said Jenny.

"You mustn't get dirty, Jasper!"

Jasper stayed clean all morning. But, as they left for the Pet Show, it started raining.

Then, ZOOM! A cat ran in front of them and tripped Jenny up. She dropped Jasper's lead.

Jasper went racing after the cat.

He ran across the wet grass and fell into the pond. SPLASH!

Come back, Jasper!

Jenny ran after Jasper and slipped on the wet grass. She nearly ended up in the pond too!

"Oh, Jasper!" Jenny cried. "Look at you!"

"Woof!" Jasper replied sadly.

Jenny tried to dry Jasper with her jumper.

It was no good – he was too wet and messy.

Now he would never win a prize for being

beautiful!

Maybe Jasper could still win the obstacle course?

There were lots of pets at the Pet Show.

Everyone smiled when they saw Jasper.

Jenny smiled back. He did look kind of cute...

But the obstacle course wasn't like the one at home. The other dogs barked and put Jasper off.

Jasper ran around the hoop instead of jumping through it.

He refused to go into the tunnel.

But at least he made everyone laugh.

At the end of the show, Jenny waited for

the judges to say who had won.

Jasper didn't come third... or second...

Then the winner was announced. But it wasn't Jasper. Jenny tried not to cry as she stroked him.

"It wasn't your fault," she told him.

"You tried your best."

And then she looked up. The mayor was walking towards her.

"Well done!" he said. And then he gave her a big silver cup!

Jenny smiled as a man took a photo of her and Jasper. What was happening?

"Congratulations, Jasper!" said the mayor. "You have won the prize for the dog who looks most like their owner."

When Jenny saw the photo, she gasped. It was true! They did look the same – wet, dirty and happy. They even had the same type of weed in their curly, blonde hair.

Jenny was so proud that people thought she looked like her lovely dog.

"Oh Jasper!" she said, hugging him.

"You really are the best dog in the world!"

Quiz

1. What did Jenny teach Jasper?
a) Jump, roll, speak
b) Left, right, paw
c) Sit, stay, come

2. What did Jasper hate?
a) Being brushed
b) Having a bath
c) Walking

3. Why did Jasper run off?
a) He was chasing a cat
b) He smelt food
c) He was chasing a ball

4. Why did everyone smile when they saw Jasper?

a) He ran away

b) He rolled around

c) He was cute

5. What prize did Jenny and Jasper win?

a) Best in show

b) The messiest dog

c) The dog who looks most like its owner

Turn over for answers

Book Bands for Guided Reading

The Institute of Education book banding system is a scale of colours that reflects the various levels of reading difficulty. The bands are assigned by taking into account the content, the language style, the layout and phonics. Word, phrase and sentence level work is also taken into consideration.

Maverick Early Readers are a bright, attractive range of books covering the pink to white bands. All of these books have been book banded for guided reading to the industry standard and edited by a leading educational consultant.

To view the whole Maverick Readers scheme, visit our website at

www.maverickearlyreaders.com

Or scan the QR code above to view our scheme instantly!

Quiz Answers: 1c, 2b, 3a, 4c, 5c